ALOHA, CHICALI!
WE HOPE THAT YOU
ENJOY THIS HAWAIIAN
TALE AND THAT YOU
LEARN SOME HAWAIIAN
WORDS.
WITH OUR LOVE,
GRANDMA DEEDIE
AND
GRANDPA CHUCK
♡

MAY 2007

Published and distributed by

ISLAND HERITAGE
PUBLISHING

94-411 KŌʻAKI STREET, WAIPAHU, HAWAIʻI 96797
ORDERS: (800) 468-2800 • INFORMATION: (808) 564-8800
FAX: (808) 546-8877 • www.islandheritage.com

ISBN: 0-89610-447-8
First Edition, Third Printing-2006

LEHUA
A LEGEND OF OLD HAWAI'I

Written and Illustrated
by
Dietrich Varez

ISLAND HERITAGE

When the volcano goddess Pele first came to Hawai'i, her great voyaging canoe stopped at a tiny island west of Kaua'i.

It was already late in the afternoon, and a beautiful sunset colored the sky.

"Let's go ashore and see if we can find some food and water," Pele said to her sister Hi'iaka. "Maybe we can even make a fire and spend the night."

Hi'iaka agreed. "You fix the fire and I'll find some food," she said. The sisters dropped the canoe's huge stone anchor and went ashore.

2

Pele loved to make fires. By the time Hiʻiaka returned with some *weke* fish and bananas, a huge blaze was going.

"It doesn't have to be so big," Hiʻiaka complained, but Pele was entranced by the red flames and hardly heard her younger sister. Pele always got that way near fire.

While Pele roasted the food, Hiʻiaka sang and danced a *hula* for her sister.

The girls stayed up late that night and told stories by the fire. Then Hiʻiaka made them a bed of fern leaves and they went to sleep.

As everyone knows, when you eat *weke* fish you will have all kinds of dreams. And Hi'iaka had been so hungry that she ate four *weke*.

Hi'iaka had hardly fallen asleep when her dream began. She saw a beautiful young girl with a little reddish brown pig. The piglet was full of energy and in good spirits. But the beautiful girl was not happy and seemed to be searching for something.

"Wake up! You're having a nightmare," Pele shouted, shaking her sister awake. "I told you not to eat so many *weke*. When will you learn?" she scolded Hi'iaka.

In the morning Hi'iaka told the dream to Pele.

"I saw the sad girl right there in that spot," said Hi'iaka, pointing to a huge rectangular rock slab.

"That's no ordinary stone," Pele said right away. "Someday it will decide the fate of chiefs or even kings," she said. "Now that this great stone has appeared in your dream, we must leave an offering to show our respect."

The sisters solemnly placed a bright red *lehua lei* on the great stone. We know that this really happened because ever since the island has been named Lehua Island.

5

Pele and Hi'iaka left Lehua Island that very afternoon.

As their great canoe Honuaiākea faded into the distance, a truly amazing thing happened.

The red *lehua lei* on the immense stone slab began to glow and change shape. It turned into a mist over the stone. There was a form in the mist. You could see it.

And when the famed winds of Lehua Island had finally blown the mist away from the great stone, the form was clear for all to see.

It was the beautiful girl of Hi'iaka's dream.

Her name was Lehua and this is her story.

Lehua slowly opened her eyes and saw a distant *heiau* or temple. An old grim *kahuna* was chanting loudly and Lehua could hear the drum and smell the smoke. There was going to be a sacrifice.

Near the huge fire was a little red piglet all bundled in ti leaves and tied up. Lehua felt sorry for the little pig and secretly set it free when no one was looking.

The pig was grateful, and they quickly stuffed a nearby feather helmet into the ti-leaf bundle and then ran for the forest.

When the old grim *kahuna* finally stopped his chant he picked up the ti-leaf bundle and flung it into the flames. He didn't realize he was actually burning the king's new feather helmet instead of the little pig.

For this insult to the king, the *kahuna* was punished. As the king's guards came to take him away, he shouted a curse with his last breath:

"Let those who caused this to befall me never be happy again until they find the happy fisherman who never catches fish and never goes to sea."

Then he died.

Meanwhile Lehua and the little pig remained hidden in the forest. Lehua had named the piglet 'Ehu, after his reddish brown hair.

"I have an uncle on the Big Island," said 'Ehu. "Maybe we could hide with him until this trouble is over. Besides, if that *kahuna's* curse ever finds you, you'll be very unhappy," added 'Ehu.

Lehua and 'Ehu quietly crept to the beach where Honu the giant turtle lived. They told Honu their story.

"Do you think you could give us a ride to the Big Island?" they asked Honu in a whisper.

"Of course," replied Honu. "I was just going there myself. Hop on and hold tight."

The trip to the Big Island was absolutely thrilling. Honu surfed one great wave after another, and soon the island appeared like a giant whale spouting a red lava plume.

But life at 'Ehu's uncle's house was not so thrilling. The uncle was a rough and scruffy fellow who kept late hours and was constantly in trouble. His name was Kamapua'a.

To make matters even worse, the dead *kahuna's* curse had found Lehua. She was now always sad and searching for happiness.

Kamapua'a let Lehua and 'Ehu have a little corner in his foul-smelling cave. But when Lehua finally asked him where she might find happiness he got very angry.

"Not here," he said shortly. "There's a house-full of girls in the forest at Paliuli above here. Take the trail from Kea'au on up to Kapu'euhi. Look for the rainbow. Their house is right under it. They might be able to help you."

Lehua and 'Ehu were up early the next morning and took the trail winding its way to the place called Paliuli.

"I love my uncle," said 'Ehu, "but he can be very hard to live with." Lehua agreed.

After a while 'Ehu put his nose in the air and was smelling something. "I think my friend Pepeiao the tree fungus lives nearby. He is the ear of the forest and hears everything."

"Good," said Lehua. "Perhaps we can ask Pepeiao where to find this mysterious fisherman who will break the curse of unhappiness. It's wearing me out."

"We're getting closer," said 'Ehu. "The scent of Pepeiao is getting stronger all the time and it is making me very hungry. Let's hurry!"

'Ehu was right. Around the very next ridge was an old *kukui* nut tree with a huge brown *pepeiao akua* growing on it.

This *pepeiao akua* was very smart and knew just about everything. He had heard it all.

"Yes, I heard the curse," said Pepeiao, "but this is really a matter of seeing rather than hearing. Furthermore, I suspect there is some trickery involved in the curse. I can't imagine any fisherman being happy if he never catches any fish. Sounds like a riddle to me. Why don't you check with Pueo the owl. He sees everything, even at night."

Lehua and 'Ehu thanked Pepeiao for the advice. Pepeiao then gave himself to 'Ehu as food.

The little pig slowly and respectfully ate Pepeiao and he could feel himself getting smarter with every bite.

'Ehu was still burping from the generosity of Pepeiao when they found Pueo the owl nodding in his tree.

"Sorry to disturb you, Pueo, but we're looking for the happy fisherman who never catches fish and never goes to sea," said Lehua. "Do you think you can help us?"

Pueo pondered the question with his eyes closed. He was using all of his wisdom and shifted from one foot to the other a few times.

"The *kahuna's* curse is in the form of a riddle which you must solve," said Pueo from his perch in a yellow *'ōhi'a* tree.

"I only see things from above and can't help you. But you must keep looking and you will surely find the answer. Try 'Enuhe the caterpillar. He gets under everything."

It was the steady munching of sweet potato leaves that gave 'Enuhe away. Otherwise Lehua and 'Ehu would never have found him. His camouflage was flawless.

"Sorry to hear you're so unhappy," said 'Enuhe, "but please don't bother me now. This is my happiest moment because I'm getting ready to die."

"That makes you happy?" asked Lehua in disbelief.

"Of course," said 'Enuhe. "You see, when I'm reborn I'll be a beautiful moth to fly about wherever I want. No more of this crawling and creeping around under stuff."

'Ehu and Lehua looked at each other as 'Enuhe ate even more sweet potato leaves and laughed until he died.

Lehua then suggested they rest for a while by a pool of water formed by a mountain stream.

14

As Lehua and 'Ehu sat by the pool of water, a goby fish came to the surface to feed upon some fallen *lehua* blossoms floating in the water.

"It might be wise to ask 'O'opu the goby fish if he can help us," said Lehua. "'O'opu is, after all, a fish and may have seen the fisherman we seek."

"Yes, but 'O'opu is under the water and we're up here. How will he hear us?" asked 'Ehu looking about for help. Suddenly he saw a grove of bamboo nearby. He had found a way to speak with 'O'opu.

'Ehu carefully chewed off a length of bamboo and stuck one end of the hollow tube into the water. Then he and Lehua began their conversation with 'O'opu through the tube.

'O'opu proved a great conversationalist and was delighted to hear from them, but was not much help with the riddle.

'O'opu's inability to help solve the riddle and break the curse caused Lehua to sadden even more.

"We've tried everything," she cried, "and no one can help us. I'm about ready to give up." 'Ehu was starting to feel a little unhappy too now. They both sat there by the water in total silence.

As if to accompany their melancholy, a melodious sweet music suddenly surrounded them. It seemed to be coming from a nearby fern grotto.

'Ehu and Lehua parted the ferns and there sat a young girl playing on a little trumpet made of ti leaves.

"My name is Kahala and I live here with the Rainbow Princess and the Maile sisters," said the girl, laying aside her little trumpet.

"You can come to our house and stay with us for a while but first we'll have to sing a song together to put us in a better mood." And then they sang to the ti-leaf trumpet.

They were still singing when they reached a large clearing in the forest. Lehua gasped when she saw the house where Kahala lived with her friends. It was the most beautiful house you could ever imagine. And it was thatched entirely with bright yellow bird feathers. A brilliant rainbow arched over the roof and the place seemed very magical.

"This is where I live now," said Kahala. "Our brother abandoned us in this forest to live in hollow trees, but the Rainbow Princess was kind enough to take us in to live with her. We have made a vow never to separate."

"Come along and I'll introduce you to the other girls," said Kahala as they approached the beautiful yellow feather house.

The radiant Rainbow Princess and the four Maile sisters were all very friendly too. And everyone really loved 'Ehu.

Lehua told of her search for the answer to the riddle and the girls were very sympathetic.

"We will try to help you," said the Rainbow Princess. "But today we were planning to go to the beach at Hilo Bay for some fun in the water. Why don't you come with us. Someone there might know of this puzzling fisherman."

Lehua and 'Ehu agreed to go. It cheered them up to find their new friends so eager to help.

18

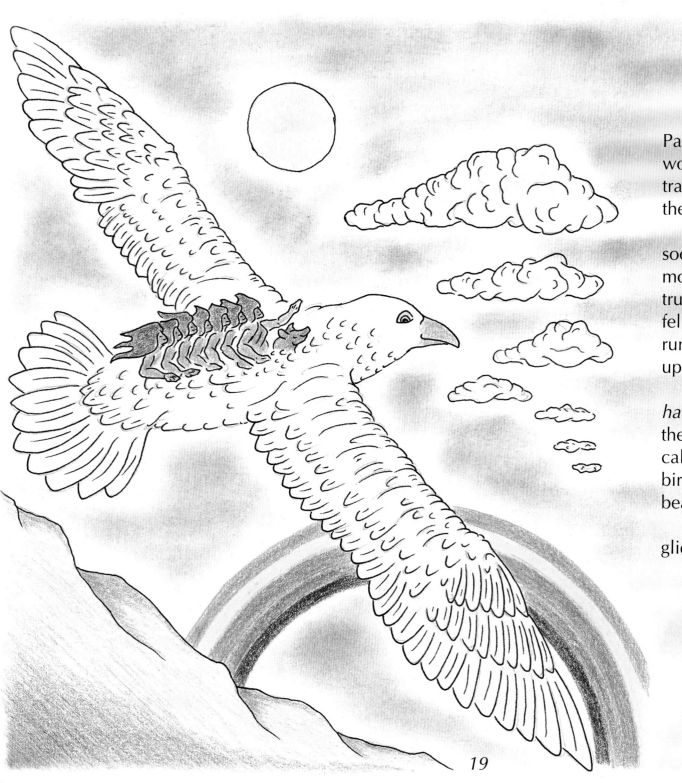

It's a long way from Paliuli to Hilo and Lehua wondered how the girls could travel so far just to play at the beach.

But that problem was soon solved. Kahala blew once more on her magic ti-leaf trumpet and a great shadow fell over them. 'Ehu started to run for cover and Lehua looked up to see what it was.

It was the legendary *halulu* bird which protected the girls at Paliuli. Kahala had called the fearsome but loyal bird to carry them down to the beach at Hilo.

It was a smooth and easy glide to the ocean.

19

Halulu let the girls and 'Ehu off at the beach and then flew back up to his secret place in the heavens.

'Ehu did a little surfing while Lehua asked all the fishermen at the shoreline her question. None of them knew the answer. But Lehua was mysteriously attracted to the fisherman who was throwing his net over some fish. Somehow she felt there was a clue here to solving the curse. She recalled 'O'opu's comment about fishing nets: "So full of holes but no way out."

Lehua too felt ensnared in the web of the riddle-curse.

The other girls were cheering 'Ehu's skillful surfing style as Lehua paused by a rocky tide pool which extended under a lava ledge.

The beach sand was very hot from the sun, so Lehua dangled her feet in the cool tide pool. She was feeling the strong grip of the curse again when something suddenly moved in the tide pool. Something big.

Lehua tried to get up but could not pull her leg free. Puhi the giant eel had wound his long body around Lehua's foot and was holding her down.

Lehua struggled to free her foot but Puhi would not let go.

Soon 'Ehu came to see what all the noise was about. He didn't dare to go near the giant *puhi* and ran to find the girls for help. But the girls were all out surfing in the waves and could not hear his calls.

21

Lehua saw that no one was coming to help her. She called out to ʻŌpae the shrimp, Pūpū the shell fish, and even Kūpeʻe the snail for help. But they were afraid to come near Puhi.

Only ʻOpihi the limpet was not afraid and came to save Lehua. ʻOpihi clamped himself over the eyes of Puhi and blinded the great eel. Then Lehua escaped.

The blind puhi thrashed about the tide pool in a rage. He tied himself into such a tight knot that he would spend the rest of his life trying to untie himself.

And Pīmoe the *ulua* fish took advantage of Puhi's blindness. Pīmoe swam by regularly to take a bite out of Puhi.

Lehua and ‘Ehu lived with the girls at Paliuli for a while longer and then decided to move on.

"We're sorry that we can't help solve your riddle and lift the curse of unhappiness," said Kahala. "But why don't you try to find your aunt Pele who lives uphill from us at the place called Kīlauea. She knows this island very well and may be able to help you."

Lehua and ‘Ehu took the advice and left for Kīlauea the next morning.

As the trail neared the rainy place called Kapu‘euhi, Lehua and ‘Ehu passed by the house of a curious fellow who was known for making ‘ohe kāpala or printing stamps. He lived there in isolation with his wife and some dogs and was prone to philosophizing.

The old printmaker's place was very quiet. He was probably inside and working in a trance on some new design. And as this odd fellow did not want to come out and is of no further consequence to this story, we will leave him to his work and move on.

Lehua and 'Ehu reached Kīlauea late in the evening. It was already dark. But they had no problem finding Pele. They followed the red glow and soon saw the volcano goddess. She was probing among some giant cracked stone slabs with Pāoa, her famed digging stick.

With each thrust of the great stick, more and more red hot lava oozed out.

24

Pele was so engrossed in her work that she did not see 'Ehu and Lehua approach.

"I think we'd better wait until morning to speak with her. She looks pretty scary tonight," said Lehua. 'Ehu agreed and they slept on the warm lava nearby.

The next morning Pele looked less fiery and Lehua introduced herself. Lehua told her Aunt Pele why she had come.

Pele recalled leaving the *lehua lei* on the little island but the volcano goddess could not answer the riddle. And Hi'iaka could not help. She was away on an errand for Pele.

Then Pele cooked a great feast for them in one of her steam vents.

"Tomorrow we'll go to the *hōlua* sledding contest," said Pele to her guests.

The crowd at the sledding meet cheered wildly for the young chief from Puna. So far he had beaten everyone at sliding down the steep slope.

Disguising herself as an ordinary woman, Pele approached the chief and challenged him to a race.

"This is not for little girls or women," he laughed at Pele. Then he threw himself on his sled and sped down the slide.

No one can insult Pele like that. She changed back into her fiery self. Pele lunged after the cocky young chief with a flow of red hot lava. She almost caught him.

The chief realized he had offended Pele. When he got to the bottom he did not come back to the slide. He ran to the sea and escaped to another island.

26

"I love my aunt Pele but she sure can be temperamental," said Lehua to 'Ehu as they watched Pele chasing the frightened chief.

Pele's eruptive behavior ended the *hōlua* contest. After the volcano goddess had cooled down she came back to sit with 'Ehu and Lehua.

"Sometimes these young chiefs need a lesson in humility," Pele apologized for her outburst. "And that reminds me," she said to 'Ehu, "if you see your uncle Kamapua'a, tell him to stop by and see me sometime. We have some unfinished business to settle."

And with that they walked over to Kīpuka-pua-ulu, where a very important ceremony was beginning. Two huge *koa* trees were to be cut for a canoe-building project.

The trees were very beautiful. They had been hand-cultivated by four generations of gardeners appointed to care for them. They even had secret names by which the gardener could speak to them.

'Elepaio the fly-catcher bird had declared the trees to be ready. He had personally inspected them for worm damage and found none.

"They're ready," said 'Elepaio to the gardener.

"Good. Here are their replacements. Harvest one, plant one," said the old gardener holding two new young seedlings.

Then the great trees were blessed and asked to become sound canoes.

They agreed.

The work to cut and hollow the long logs began as the old gardener planted the new seedlings.

'Elepaio told the canoe makers where the bow and stern should be on each log. The great canoes slowly began to take shape in a sea of wood chips.

Then all the work stopped and more ceremonies began. The unfinished hull would now be skidded down to the seashore for completion.

"If everything is done correctly the hulls will find their own way down to the seashore. That's how eager they are to become canoes," said 'Elepaio.

Lehua and 'Ehu soon learned what that meant. They sat in one of the hulls as it skidded full speed down the mountain to the beach and came to rest in the soft sand.

In a long canoe shed, the twin hulls were bound together into a voyaging canoe. No time was wasted and the great canoe was soon ready for launching.

"The way everyone is hurrying to build this canoe it must be for something very important," 'Ehu observed.

"Perhaps we should stay here to see what it is that requires such a huge canoe,"

Lehua answered.

After the canoe sailed away, Lehua and 'Ehu lived in the empty canoe shed waiting for the boat to return.

In forty days a sail appeared on the horizon and the canoe came back into Hilo Bay.

Lehua and 'Ehu ran to meet the boat as it anchored. They could not believe what it was carrying.

It was the immense rock slab on which Pele and Hi'iaka had placed the *lehua lei*. The stone on which Lehua had been born.

The canoe sat very low in the water under the weight of the heavy stone. Lehua watched as the men dragged the huge boulder off the canoe and up the beach to a special place.

Lehua was stunned to see the stone but did not go near it. There were many onlookers and also some warriors and chiefs present, but they paid no attention to the little girl with her pet pig.

Something very important was going to take place.

It was then that Lehua saw the crowd part and become very quiet as a tall chief stepped out.

He had a kind but determined face. He passed Lehua, smiled and reached down to pet ʻEhu a few times as if he were going to need some good luck.

The crowd parted for him as he approached the great stone. He paused before the boulder and laid his hand on it. He appeared to introduce himself.

"If he doesn't lift it they will kill him," said someone in the crowd. Some warriors with long, sharp spears were already nearby, waiting for the chief to fail.

"But if he lifts it, he'll be King," said another. There were attendants ready with the royal cloak and feather helmet, should he succeed.

The chief spit in his hand for grip and seized one end of the boulder. His feet sank into the soft sand as he strained against the stone.

Silence fell over the crowd. All eyes were on the chief and the immense stone.

He began to lift but sank in the sand up to his ankles under the weight. The great stone would not move and only settled itself deeper in the sand.

Lehua and 'Ehu watched intently. They felt sympathy for the young chief and hoped he would succeed.

The chief strained against the weight once again. As he exerted himself, his eyes caught Lehua's face in the crowd. Lehua wished with all her might that he would be able to lift the stone. She seemed to have a mysterious power over the boulder because it suddenly began to rise.

The crowd cheered wildly as the straining chief stood the stone straight up and then, with one last great effort, pushed it over.

Now he was King.

A colorful celebration followed. And no one knew why the new King ordered Lehua and 'Ehu to sit with him at the coronation feast. They were his guests of honor.

"I know it was you and 'Ehu who helped me to lift the stone," the King whispered to Lehua.

"It's the stone I was born on," Lehua whispered back. "That stone knows me." And Lehua told about the curse and riddle.

"As you were kind enough to help me, I will now help you," said the King. "I myself cannot resolve the riddle, but my personal *kahuna* is the most skillful in all the islands. He will know the solution."

Then the King called for his *kahuna* to sit with them at the feast. 'Ehu and Lehua liked this wise old man right away. And they all soon became very good friends.

34

The King's *kahuna* carefully listened to Lehua's story about the riddle and the curse. Riddles were his specialty. No one could fool him.

When Lehua had finished her story the old man smiled at her and said, "Of course I know the answer, but it won't do for me to tell it to you. The riddle is meant for you alone to solve. But I can tell you where to find the answer."

Lehua and 'Ehu were very excited by his words and hoped the curse would soon be lifted. They were both already beginning to feel happier.

Sitting there among the trees and flowers, the old man gave a soft whistle and a very beautiful 'ō'ō bird appeared.

"'Ō'ō will show you where to look. Follow him," the old man told them.

35

The bird was easy to follow because of his distinct yellow and black markings. Lehua recalled the wonderful house of the Rainbow Princess which was made entirely of yellow 'ō'ō feathers.

On the fourth day the bird landed. And no matter what 'Ehu or Lehua did, the 'ō'ō would not go further.

"The bird is trying to tell us something," said Lehua, looking about for a clue. 'Ehu was also scurrying about looking.

The four days of following the 'ō'ō bird had worn them all out so they decided to rest a while beneath the *naupaka* bush on which the bird was perched.

"I just know the answer to our riddle is right around here," said Lehua. "I can feel it."

In the silence of that spot Lehua and 'Ehu sat looking at each other. A lone fly buzzed by and landed on a leaf of the *naupaka* bush.

Suddenly from the underside of the leaf, a very curious yellow spider leaped out. In an instant the spider had thrown its net over the unsuspecting fly.

Lehua and 'Ehu looked closer at the spider. It was then that they both knew this was the answer to the riddle. The spider had the markings of a happy face on its back.

This was obviously the happy fisherman who never caught fish and never went to sea. The very rare and seldom-seen happy-face spider only uses its net to fish for flies in the forest.

The riddle was solved. The curse was lifted.

It was easy to see that Lehua and 'Ehu had regained their happiness.

They danced around the *naupaka* bush until sunset. And the 'ō'ō bird sang his very best songs for them until dark.

They stayed up real late recalling moments of their fantastic adventure and how they would never forget it. Then they all fell asleep in the ferns.

And that is the legend of Lehua and her friend 'Ehu and their search for happiness. It is finished. The end. *Pau*.

Glossary of Hawaiian Words

'ehu	reddish-brown hair of Polynesians
'elepaio	species of bird, believed to be goddess of canoe makers
'enuhe	caterpillar
halulu	to roar, thunder, make a loud noise
heiau	place of worship
Hi'iaka	Pele's youngest sister
Hilo	city and bay on the island of Hawai'i
hōlua	ancient sled used on grassy slopes
honu	turtle or tortoise
hula	dance
kahuna	priest
Kamapua'a	ancient Hawaiian pig demigod
Kapu'euhi	land section, now Glenwood, Puna, Hawai'i
Kea'au	land section/village in Puna, Hawai'i
Kīlauea	active volcano on the island of Hawai'i
Kīpuka-pua-ulu	park near Kīlauea, Hawai'i
koa	native forest tree with fine red wood formerly used for canoes
kukui	candlenut tree, official emblem of the state of Hawai'i
kūpe'e	marine snail

lehua	flower of the ʻōhiʻa tree
lei	necklace given as a symbol of affection, usually of flowers
maile	a native twining shrub
naupaka	native shrub with white or light-colored flowers
ʻohe kāpala	printing or stamping a design using carved bamboo
ʻōhiʻa	tree or shrub with red, pink, yellow or white flowers
ʻōʻō	bird, a black honey eater with yellow feathers under each wing, extinct
ʻoʻopu	general name for fish in the goby family
ʻōpae	general name for shrimp
ʻopihi	limpet, marine life with cone-like shells that cling to rocks
Paliuli	legendary paradise of plenty in Puna, Hawaiʻi
pāoa	divining rod or staff used by Pele to test the earth
pau	finished, ended
Pele	volcano goddess
pepeiao	ear, to hear
pepeiao akua	tree fungus, the Jew's-ear
pueo	Hawaiian short-eared owl
puhi	eel
Puna	land section in southeast Hawaiʻi
pūpū	general name for shells, tiny shell beads
ulua	jack, important game fish and food item
weke	fish, popular as offering to gods